RETROCEDE

ISBN: 978-1-916541-06-1
First edition.

This book is a work of fiction.

First published in 2024 by Erratum Press
Sheffield, UK
www.erratumpress.com

Design and typesetting by Ansgar Allen
Paintings by Michael Mc Aloran

RETROCEDE

Michael Mc Aloran

ERRATUM PRESS

"I remember looking at a dog-shit on the pavement and
I suddenly realized, there it is - this is what life is like.
Strangely enough, it tormented me for months, till I came
to, as it were, accept that here you are, existing for a second,
brushed off like flies on the wall."

Francis Bacon

...from out of which...the dead tones of a broken shadow a prism's eclipt a nocturne of the flayed carcass of breathe forgive it shit in the veins of having ever...

shattered glass oxide a turning in the meat of sarcophagus tears breathless to touch where blood's spasm is nothing of the closure of it fleshed upon...

ever the traceless defunct light cascading into some other realm...the endless night rising in the parched throat what callous where turns the other cheek and is merely met with further emptiness...

here a commence...the birthing & the of it a strip of jouissance collision ember in the dark to utter flame that ever of what will broken throughout whispering unto the naught of ever-absence...

it was spat/ shale blessed the cut of the bone in the palms of children lost to the night's cascade...here the winds of it forgotten close the door there is no other route...

unto to step beyond throughout what breathe into some foreign another where the ever bites what closure closer sharp another room another frenzy...

it dug deep the pit…& the lie of the flesh marred by sycophantic absences pissing upon in vacancy where never of the blood's aligned what damage through seasons dead as a lie was broken bread & the hyenic flay of tongues whispering of the speech irredeem…

as nothing of…the silence eradicates & all that was what with silken pageant of null stricken from the book a fist a fucking avarice there is nothing here to see…

amber lights to shred in the nothing ever other what… in a mirror of unto night is a forest of spent bones lacking in the butchery of dementia silences…

walls through which nothing is visible other than the blockade of never of…it has spoken colourless till dreamt of in a silver adagio of frozen tide…

in a mirror of ever till absenteeism is the obsolete as the reek of blood's colossus stretches to the corners of the skyline's abortive malady…

nothing ever spoken from nor which of will null & void what matter of close the binding wound till drift undone…

taking back from out of the outstretched hand where blood is syllabus...confetti of flaked breathe a scattering of circus animus...lapse then shadow of...

paranoiacal exigency struck out by opiate discharge... glass shatter of in the absence of redeem upon which to kneel till drift along forgotten in the horror of till collapse a dead breath nothing ever having other than...

time measured out in...seconds pulsating as of blood from an open wound...the taste writhes deep into collectively eradicating the collisioned what savage ever nothing said of ever-else...

a razor a letting of crimson cells nothing more where gilted the flesh frozen in the scar tissue of smiles long forgotten closure as...till build of flame what spill...

it has been before ever in the of what speech butchered as be done what wind in it forgotten absent fingers shredded by the silence of some vacated roomscape of soldered absent...

a killer's teeth mark the pathway to the knife's edge where to closure of in haste is the broken outspoken... close the wound...

nothing of the never of the nothing of frozen as was before...where spinal is the warped tongue caressing within the broken body vocal...

colours drip from walls blind-sighted in a shadowy frozen malice...as lapse what of through ember gladiolae none what spoke of null the severed fingers of dis-ease...

it is dead see eye see nothing of the words that mark the terrains of nothing ever...laughter breathing into the corrupt lung where sickness haven strikes the nullity of foreign excrement given as...

speech climbs in the valves of nowhereon as if to ask of what of nothing the bereft of...till closure eyes of the expelled diameter where breakage bone is the night's kiss an empty travail...

sudden as if to devour till lack wither in the haven speech colourless attrition nestle in marrow what have you...it stun breakage...piss upon the flame...

till sudden as if to echo-echo nothing of the redeem... upon one knee...bent into some apparent worship where to breathe is to foreign in realms of attrition ever-as...

walls burn in the aftermath the premise the in of where being in is the rat shit closure of forgotten ever…blank spaces shattered fingers & the meat of distance seek where null & void…

it is lung the breakage valve whereof what spun in tint of measure seamless to collide…it or what in of where silence broken valves of feel till suck upon dry bones no here there or of hereafter…

flesh to peel away the abject nullity the extol of concave evisceration…all as if to having where nothing claim it a lapse a vacancy where having been closed wound an accurate sheen…outspeak of.…

& a collapse of depth where never was…stripped bare by assassin winds the cauterized never heals/ it…as unto oceanic ever of to flow submerged colours the light by which none is forever undivided…as if to…

drag out the reek of time to some other realm…a slipstream nothingness of abortive flex…extracted the bones culled from some collapse of never having never yet will other than…

& all as if forgotten…nothing to see here move along… skeletal breath a sickness of deliverance ripped from the inside out by some collapse of detritus a frozen picture postcard until unto…

unto through the depth what obsolete disaster…broken tines of words scattered toward the depth of a forgotten skyline…dead what of there or other the little that calls from respite…black labyrinth…spits it out as of bloody phlegm…

======================================

…a headless descent of scattered tongues burn into sands the light by which is severed closes the night's chamber to electric absence bitten goes the words that close no woundage…

…it-spoke till draft what closure spasm effortless the skull cracks beneath the weight of the dawn till extricate silence of the bleed of eye the momentary afflict…

…all footsteps eradicated…swept aside the films of having ever of…trace will limb diseased the flow of bitter aftermath where the children scatter the scars of tide into some other neither the of nor other…

…rat bite down what echoing veranda of clear cut blood is the dischase of splinter havoc till turn of dawning in the titanium abort…

…it all undone marking the pelt of nothing spread out before the cataract eyes till peeled away a dragoon of bread broken nothing of till savour call…

…it light it a shattered lightbulb as inhaled the stench of foreign waste in the silence…words crack till speech eradicate nothing of the install into a bared to the sky whereof the bite the sheen till taint of nethertheless…

...it is undone...amphetamine overtures & the adrift of sudden shock shadow-lapse...tone deaf the hollow skull bends into or never of close the lips where circuit spasm is the beneath of animal foraging into the meat cast off from the body vocal a broken semblance...

...it is of the undone till waver breakage nothing of the before where the carousel of breathe is the sickness of haven rot closed down nothing of a door made of sand an hourglass settlement knock once it dissipate a shredded lung & the break of desolate...

...as all till turn of nothing fragrant as the decay of ever-sky falling lack it grace a trance a broken column a wrench from the emptily skull depth as was once utter now...reduced to...

...till exit all the while a breakage of the exorcism a candle extinguish in the breathe of breath throughout the density of the rind...not nor of what matter throughout...cold chamber ever left behind only to reappear...

...dead tones of echo-drought...no sun was ever of through warms no flesh forgotten/ cannot...collapsed into where specious the tide that coats the ruptured meat is of a shadow of what once was till trace what of ever of the recall...

…there is skin & there is nothing of the bone till bind of night yet never beyond where which…it casts dice in deserted alleyways as if to murmur it was never of…

…sheet metal snaps down a doorway a snare a cracked window smeared with shit till seepage of marrow the seared eye of nocturne of broken bones…unseen unsung in a swarm of carrion flies till seepage rot of putrid meat where sickness of till dredge collapse of psychosis bleeding the corpus underbelly…

…it what in or nor of a density of nothing that cannot be quantified…extracts the fingernails in the dark where closure of the final door ablaze…it what lapse…

…grasp the…sears flesh…grasps the…opens unto spe/ cial of cylindrical promise a room alone a penny arcade to rot within…

…unto as if to spoken heave of the gutter gullet of the unto ever lapse a closure of emblems of night break stun depth till tread eye alone as if to echo-dream a closure of tongues nothing of some implosion a careless aside…

…a rip a night of…a caress of light & the butchery of broken words scattered like dogshit…dread to stir in the skull laughter of in or of all the forgotte…

…dead once it utters of the ever-breathing onslaught unto…slashed out the gait is a silver glint a breakage point of nothing ever of respoke wounds as if to tread where eye expel of taint of orchid distances…

…not a bloody chance from outset once…it suffocates & tears the wings of the sky to pieces…pissed upon in furtive stagnation where viscous the air is of the lapse all night's devour in the exigent of having never…

…walls to trace in the half-light candle-lit a cupped hand offering forth is filled with maggot swarm the breakage lapse of catacomb desire…till taste… irredempt of…

…till gutter tread spread-eagled across burning of the pale light searing into nothing ever…trace dull tide of…

…absolve collect breakage bones a vacuum of forgotten realms scattering the eviscerated till lie alone in the vast the tread extract the teeth of malady whereof till sky alone will never of a semblance a nocturne a…

…a-breathe till shadow-form of spent sound corrosively tearing into breathless…the dead speech taking nothing from the nothing of…all sense devoured…

…*burning shit in crumpled black swan paper…dead of…never of what will throughout it spoken limbs to warp in some forgettable excise…till list of breakage…*

…*spill of fuck & the absent body licking the wounds till closure tabulet shattered to the marrow a corrupt night emblem lack nothing left to trace as the fingers search for promise of the abortive skyline suck it down like opiate smoke…*

…*till laugh alone…alone is the word of ever in the midst the sarcophagus of being in where to be to to dissolve a frozen wound in the nothing of a closure null & voidal of till what…*

…*as spoken again as if to having spoken again as if to nothing ever…dead what once once more…a mirror peeling away to reveal as…eye asks of the never having…*

…*callused fingers once will tread till speak of denizen of a shear of razor clemency separating the naught from the marrowing…it eye done…door slams shut once more…*

…*a clear wind flecked with blood breaks throughout till frozen baseless forgotte deaf unto…as if to say that the laughter returns…thereof…*

…frozen in the flesh of it as if to semblance nothing of throughout…till lapse…till pass around the razor slash of skin severed of the benign…a glut….a solace…bled out nothing further ever null & spent…till dream of… cauterized…as all…

=====================================

excise whereof from wound was stripped collapse into thy nullity of breathe's dissolve a taste of blood in the mouth in out-reaching seethe of nectar havoc a scattering of limbs dead cold ice-white alarm…

till fallen exigent through where to sleep is to absence of in a pit of razor-bound tillage of the pulse bulb reckless to shred where bone attrition a nectar exhale colourless static in the eye that once was ever-no of the absurd forgot reflected in the pupil sting yet nothing of the breakage point…

the sharded light frozen where nothing of is the taint the expire the genuflect upon barren obsolete throughout where specious is the absolute & never less than one footstep forth yet unto nothing ever till retrace what will the eye upon where eye dissolve it depth what silence never once known forgotten never of…

lapse into till wrench of steel caressing the sinew the veins the light by which nothing can be seen of the echo-echo night as if to collide with broke stone never of in the non-speech the dead ends these rapture spat out cold dim in a shithouse realm the doors locked from the inside till trace what long dry air to crush & dissolve… it be…

*nothing having been throughout where a suicide of
silenced parameters is the ache the taste ever to return
a silver glint in tomb's elected nothingness where skull
alone houses the nocturne depth what solace from as if
it cannot...*

*scratch scrape this heavenly body it says never of
throughout what of no matter of throughout where
closure null long stretch of abortive cheer the breathe
aligned in some abattoir the broken chalice of closure
all forgotten as if there were never any...*

*desert of bones of ages cast to dissolve & spliced with
blood a tearing the coil that binds no mortal sheen
excises strips from skin in a redempt of nothing ever...
nothing more true...little else to scrag up to laughter-
laugh upon digs it out...*

*all walls fall it say through a film of the abort of...
cauterize the light of the cauterized the light is frozen in
shafts of dark draining the colours whole of presence...*

*it what lung & the abrasive nothing of before nor into
as if to reek/ speech lack of promise of the turning lock
a waxen key not matter a...cannot will not till stepped
alone...*

bone wrench of some desire or other as the eye perceives it cannot perceive it any further…as a meld of breakage takes from what spillage of cum upon bloody flesh…

erectile majesty called ashore back then till outstep where to burn black char of dissolute a seeker's promise eradicated breaking upon the rocks of bleak mortality… till else what of the other than where lightless the pageantry sings & the cadaver remains the corpse the bloodless flesh peering out from what there…

it all along…burned out flame of speech…of the echo-dim…melding of sickness tread till cast undone breaking upon where tide does not neither the lest there oxide tread what a scattering of the what of trace elongated bloody liquid a never to collapse into pageant of no matter…

eye as if to say that in nor of what structure dense wall accord peers out from the collapsed dead teeth scattered frugally where the children play or merely flee to the darkness of the forests of silences…what will…neither of…

nothing is happening here…or ever of…the shards pierce the fish eyes cold as neither which in an antium of blood fleeing for the shadows…as on…nothing to see here nothing ever of…scarred unto scarred cold shoulder devour in the midst of flee a raptured never of where the locked jaw is the depth of desire burning in the clotted membrane…purity struck out from the book…

dead tense what matter…peeling away the glut of carcass breathing all sensed aborted…as of in the within out…walls warp…the silence never ends…

given that was once throughout a drought a frozen room viewed through shutter snapped upon one singular footstep a bloody step nothing more to see of it…

wry bound bones warped & bound in a corridor elected to no light what whispers from the dregs of ashen promise a closed fist the mercury tide of it…silence as there never was in detritus tidal flowing nothing of cold colours the like of which devouring themselves as in to the advance of…

sees the flesh gradually falling away as if to echo once of till final null a penetrate wind taking the teeth from the edge of nothing ever skinned pit break till none never once where override a circle burns at the pathway's end…

dead light thereof the frenzy as to pillage kill of sentient close of reek in lungs settled to devour as if once said… not a trace of shadow where the womb of it being in of it cannot close the eye till tillage of cull wet blood a circuit here or there removed where it no longing bitten by hyenic laughter a breakage of collapse till shred what once…

yet the screams return as into of what matter no not a some circus dreaming of spent accord a broken avarice collecting in the parched throat where blood once nestled…waxen all…

the flesh the foraging peeling away the lightless pageantry of meat scattered to the dogs of nothingness as if to turn from which yet cannot it is of the woundage the approximate disclosure…as said what once…seethes settles in a closure of ever after nullity of the…skinned as if to…

eye cannot no longer of of the onward into nullity speaking of the dead diameters the fruitless harvest in this…no longer wishing for…peering out of the one dead eye looking for the other than where apathy's trace is malign settlement till echo once more…nothing to advance from…

nothing to be gained from…a candle slashed out leaving a bloody trace the footstep illuminated in the half-light now a distance…breakage of the rock till fore in terseless weight effortless devoid is the skull of in-dream where shadow wept & as & as if to echo staunch lights the blood of nullity till depth what end…

it is of the scattering of aborted soundings one of the other nethertheless till semblance colourless blank void a ruptured ache as if to echo were to no other than settle stone ice rock paper scissors once more till foreign bitten…

nothing of the dead that is the silent realm of speeches cast out through prism lights purposeless devour of the skull once turn a silhouette…as if to…the tongue weight… in-lacerate of some breathing lapse in the dense white air that clogs the veins some abattoir closure a confetti discharge of shards of blood…

till be no other than…no pathway turning in upon… glass shatters…it is the sunlit of dispel where to rock upon is a discharge of filament the broken object bodily expels through of…no nothing of the eye of breakage tones silt for blood sickness to close the sky to the eyes of none…

staunch what what claim as if to through some other what/ what felt throughout the eye's mimicry...dust upon spilled blood...astringent...collapse into where din of mock the salve of which till spill of emptily...

as dawn what dawn what rooms to perambulate... till closure fist of door a wreckage of bones cast dice nothing of which to sever holding the marrow of the non-utterance the silence ever of mocking the dirt of...

fragrantly disembowelled...it is of...neither the turning of the weight's back-step the blind lock of original premise where spoken is of rotting razors gathered in a desert outstretch/ of...

===

...through a slipstream of eye yes another one closure of no wound a silver intermezzo of cold colours the like of which embedded in the meat of it where matter no nothing of that closure tongue of the obtruse blade curving upon where nothing of is the forgotten split in the dim spliced light echoes of bedamned it once of forgotten emblems nothing of the like of which where gardenias flow throughout the blood of absolve relapse in a simulacrum of teeth the fleeing vortex of blood ripped from the pulse bulb excreata of silence tread what once till naught division nothing of which to consider the collapsed dread nothing of the abreast of oceanic closure of the wound the tongue cast to the shadow shale where to if but when in the of the none closure abandon lessened as if to mimicry till dance alone in the shadows of star light cast upon frozen soil it what when in laughter of intoxicate where birthed the once frozen of the divine waste what be as if to echo forgotten bold as/

nothing of that of the which collect seasons to dissolve as all fall sunderance decays throughout till drag what held where some circumference closed door another realm another opening into the flesh of having nothing ever till rapture an escape of hyenic laughter the skies ablaze with the milk tooth dust of silent children till trace what done in genuflect in the forgotten shadow till lie alone in the frenzy dark as to give preference for the object other of in which what sudden collision nothing of throughout the bind semblance unto fall scattered the dead pelt of tomorrow a scrag a measure nothing other than through eye's bankrupt needle shattering the unspoken to rust to bleached skin upon which to tread in sickness neither health nor otherwise where as if to into of the burn silence all the while collapsing the get it over with the erase it to gutterize where the none doth flow in the splendour of nothing less of being expelled where broken is the forgotten endlessly unravelling where to build is to fall distances all of merely of the surmise cold shoulder dread of the one thing further of a lacerate as each hour departs and nothing other than the breath binds blindly as if unto spoken of throughout as the drag of some corpse of being in of the rat closure piercing the meat of till dreamt of broken glass nocturne a silence of distaste where bones vibrate in the dim light kaleidoscope of burning wings a seasoning a drought skinning the eyes of pageantry sickness of till dredge a scattering of bloody ash where fingers to outreach never fully grasp devout as a slashed wrist a carrion feel of empty wordless landscapes desolate to wrenched asunder till broke stone effervescence as the mirror peels away to reveal a teaming of maggot silences reflected in the eye of nothing as breakage upon a cold oceanic of tears of shit of null & void collision breathe of dispel till lock alone as broken silences reclaim the distances *of dead tones where wordless as noted is to un-sky shat upon from outset denizen of collapse it to once yet never of sudden as if to falter before unto whereof till scatter drift in the blood-flecked winds the rat of being in of the other than no contest not a fucking chance as till nothing of of the cold shoulder a reek of acidic nullity sudden lights the broken bread of breath extracts the flesh through a syringe collapse unto thy din of forgotten blessed be the membrane eradicated from all sensory in the din of night ever-outstretched to bite down upon where the none is the vacancy of shuddering of as in throughout a working of the weight of it given to the obscure it depth what matter of no matter as if to having is closure semblance the nocturne of foreign nothing more to see of the intent as forgotten was in throughout a closure obsolete dead as a lie is a vapour trace of dis-ease till eye what done throughout in nectar of the meat of it to warp & burn in the sickness of dread's position to beseech of which to burn in ruptured solace the cold black viscid lights tearing asunder what depth till lacerate -repeats…*

close the eyes the rest will follow it done in by the flesh of it the silence a-breathe what of in dredge a shiv to the throat of measuring turning in the soil of fragrant char of words as of spent cadavers nothing to cling to nothing to silenced throughout closure of the wound the orifice of the mouth stitched across where broken sudden as if to nothing of the before till in-dreaming of a bitter weight skinned what depth of razor solace a cool clean burn a garrotted throat bile vomit piss upon the obsidian flowers of it till graven knocked from the tooth of spell a spillage of bloodless headless attrition silently divulged in an ache of being nothing as what of till nocturne's onslaught breaking from fever solace of the one thing foreign as of stolen from collapse into in the wrench of nothing ever stretching out into a vague landscape of broken effigies till suicidal teeth bared unto the bereft sun's light a rupture of lung a stretch from distant realms where to breathe is the occluded spasm specious as where bones to caress the breakage of ashen purposes spit upon a graven sudden to reclaim where declaration be as sky forgotte all walls to having in or of dissipation nothing of the before nothing of the throughout nothing of the breaking bones the shat upon lacking origin effortlessly devoured by the rat of in nor of no longer meaning as fallen into a pit of rotting shit & butchered limbs till sink in the cold haven of soundless collapse where to hence is to sudden disavowal dead tones for the redempt no sounding for the bereft of it no ending of the broken majesty of it fallen unto the transparent the mockery grin of hyenic final breath as if to ache of it were to be beyond what will dragging out the weight of it to the pregnant outstretch where worthless the design is the colour of the expelled lacking any fucking chance of severed

warped bodies scattered upon distance visible through
a crimson mist desolate the beauty of parched bones the
vicious of nullity ablaze cast silhouettes a shadowing
across the eye where to maggotling is to abandon ever
of cold weight of breathless splice a trace of nocturne
vague as silenced it what sense all sensory devoured as
to behold is to erase is to eradicate no nothing of the lie
it lays it down upon where to nothing having ever of
the abattoir of the pissoir light where plumes distaste &
where to emaciate is to the discolouring nothing of once
said a closed fist an echo nothing of aroundelay it goeth
what dreams for the hours that beat in the stripped
carcass emptiness silenced from in specious fallen by
the wayside where to brace is to having fallen given
to never having a reek of blood of carrion not a in the
dim forgotten a trace else to fill the sudden scattering of
where nothing once of ever all as spoken of irredempt
through dead eyes wandering in the lack of being in
what speech declaration throughout a closure nullity
breaking from the silenteeism an echo trail a vertigo
of ever of as if to having nothing of the bled sudden
disavowal of all that be as closed of door to electrical
cable frenzies scarlet the tone of beseech of riddle it of
where if to foreign lapse till ever the return to none of it
where shit devoured is the engrained memory given to
collide with breathe so sudden as if to nothing neither
the other of what skull froze in time's long discharge of
welts of sarcophagus tidal as was frozen walls as once

were traced with the fingertips in utter dark the absence
viscous as all that it could ever be through sickness
dredge of till close of hour lacking of the intent of given
unto as a drag of carcass feel lacking any motion in
a glimpse of non-percept as the eyes turn to dust and
masquerade as having ever of where step non-trace is
the bitten ever of till close of wound not a in some circus
dreaming the membrane in a vice of subtle colours
nothing as before where to turn it cannot into of further
fielded given to the bitten of the entrenched devour it
speak what of it nothing ever of the surmount of bones
to drag from withered lungtish of spelling it all out in
shards of frozen meat dense as shit as ever was before
yet turning of into throughout in spillage of scarlet
emptily where force what spun a candelabra made of
human bones the freshen brittle marrow into where
no precipice design as if to merely once & the rupture
of all syllabus shadowing the playground of the dead
the holier of than thou an excise of raw meat stretched
across the abyss some secretive design it of which spilling
it out as if to ravage all that was with a cold blank stare
from the rat of disclosure nothing of where next what of
as onwardly into haven lights a shudder of death-will
as onwardly no matter it of where speak what drift it
closure tongue lessened of where to exhalation bind is
the plague of retrospect nothing as before in the dim
forgotten roaming throughout the distance where to be
is pare away the bones of it netherless the blood it is

spilled a carnivore's delight when sunk white distances play upon as if to light spoken of through trilogy as on into taken from what pillage distances to trace in the acid burn of feel shear of the mebrane nothing as before as was before as having been forgotten in the dim light of nowhow on as once taken from what frenzy absolute till closure of moved to the nausea of having been before where merely to nothing ever is the deathly turning of what shaken purpose as the orchard of bone weight climbs to the hilt of the sky's line all purpose shattered calling cards as one adrift it spoke what terse it tongue as if in throughout what bite sucking down the smoke of ages unforeseen as if to inflamed where the cool caress is of the blanketing of eyes long weary of the cavalcade of the dead till turn of fruitless colourings even to touch the cold dream shattered ice through which the obsidian flowers spread as dust in lung of teasement callused the skin that works long depth of stun eclipse making a mockery of all what spent in distances collision breakage lockage avalanche of frozen tears of the biting into meat stripped of heavenly dissent nothing more valid as if to say that nothing more true than in absolute stripped till lock of final flourish as if to mockery it utters murmurs beneath the breath of disclosure it cannot in some broken verbatim of ever-of a fragmentary shell of scattered tomorrows/

dead once

it says yet dying all the while of which as if to having in the corrupt light breakage as was sudden disavowal null it cannot broken by nothing in the vague tense spillage of bile piss cum and retrospect a dense reclaim a cracked jaw leaking the forgotten of the matter merely to seek what din a foreign naught ever-changing its parameters its excise no no nothing in that till closure taint of light a vellum stretch of dissolve wreckage nothing ever held to the bone the flesh penetrated by the if nor when it has as was said till closure of in the which not have throughout listless as if to climb what sun song deaf eye spy what longing in the have of have not till silenced through amphetamine of ages sickness of which to collapse in the downpour depth of no solace an ache a tryst a breaking forth as if to having in or other climbed what of ever of till laughter long a closed fist a breakage point no distance left to tread through the what will unto the horizon where the sun's dissolve is merely nothing other than to speak of which cold shoulder a breakage point what closure night to embalm all what of it let it/ if…

===

...from the onslaught/ breathe of the raw teeth of extinction the spent laughter of foreign of some death-like pulse given to unshadow as was till never of throughout as if to utter in the collapse of skeletal lights where to having birthed once shattered glass of some ferocity skinning the night to the veins all naught as if to ever echoing throughout a vibrate of exigency shudder blind weight a sudden as if to mimicry to cut to reclaim the maggot tones of what spoken haven to scatter the pelts of long forgotten in the cancerous air as was once so shall it be till rapture ever of closed fist a-bleed sickness to dredge as was once tidal to give sudden reclaim as if to having nothing of the eye's removal a breakage point a tide of never having before witnessed merely by the reflect of the skyline's premise as was dragged in the kick & scream of bitter silences where to option is to burn to char a sudden word a semblance etched across the vellum emptily all sung from naught broke shale through the fingers to fall upon where other than no landscape worthy of the winds to clear away the meat of emaciated loveless breaking from fever pitch in sickness & in deathly-like as onward into having no course for the oppress the process lacking in progress cut stone an illuminary absence in the absentee skull as if to say as was in the beginning it has come to end to furrow to nothing more where the silence cannot breath-like in the dead tense the breakage of flesh vibrating in clear dark

*space it has walked through passageways and sought
the exit-tidal pathway dreamt of where a recourse to
having nethertheless back steps a motion of this or that
having of the forgotten nothing more to barel as if
to collide in the weight of it the shadows vane the
absolute in terse dislocation of dispel as to be in a rat's
trace a solace emptily as scar upon scar nothing of the
having ever been otherwise no vault of which to drag
from in the hung light quartered then vast as speaketh
from no distance from in elixir of burning as if to
burning unto begone as if to end were tol all vast yet
no distance to tastel*

*nothing other than to be nothing
of nor to see through cataract skin of the cataract view
of dishevelled meat burning throughout as cold spasm
taketh from the outstretched skyline in a catascope of wet
blood nocturne reek of spent lights of the dim forgotten
as circus goes the razor roundelay the bones shattered
till obsolete claim upon nothing ever of as was as if to
nectar of silenced overtures of the mebrane's kiss upon
stone nothingness bludgeoning the gait the shadow
formed & frozen upon the wall as in the mirror gazes
inwardly into where to final is to lack all manner of
which obscure as if to echo drift what dim in viscid
irredeem weightless travail in specious ever as before as
dead alone for all time a tidal wasteage of ever of till
scarred without longing skinned of ever after all turning*

*from the electrical cable frenzy of scattered orchids where
to be is to being of the rat's pulse the teeth smeared frozen
in an outwailing scream of discharge broken to become
other than in a sarcophagus of night endless where to
touch is to dissipate merely of the skin in-dream of the
lightless space where ever-as divides all sung from vast
astringent where to absence scattered the dead pelts long
forgotten into a pit of assassin lapse of final absolute ever
of until where froze wind knock upon as burn of into
of the burning to be gone throughout all dense what
will till trace redempt upon one knee genuflect before
the absence of in retrocede concession no in the sickness
of the bile rising to the throat of it blood spatter upon
a blank wall nothing of the seen nothing of the weight
nothing of the following after nothing of the hour that
pierces/*

cannot/

*as to rolling around in shattered glass
the emaciation of rat in the buried bones of membrane
where to exit signs of unspoken weight as if to shadowing
collectively the crush of spit polish nullity a matter of
fact trace through the skin's cataract where to break
unto in the absence feel of given lest it biteth amber
nocturnes of frozen grey mists in the nauseate of silence
never to expel through the static hours of skin stretched
upon as of throughout biting down upon to sever where*

to mockery is the hyenic laughter of the death-bearing tidal as as if to into from what will in which none of graceless to unto nothing of as the candied corpses mount in the cupped hands of the dawn as nothing to feel with nothing to breathe through never of the beseeched from carved into the flesh into the meat into the bones revealed where sudden as if to fall is tread without motion static as the blind lapse the utter dark the reclaim dead tones of some silver intermezzo collision pulse seeking of the out of reach till spent force no nothing of the afterward where to breakage of the shit-smeared glass of it the eyes that cannot quantify bound limbs scattered in a winter orchard of denuded exigency it is of the sung/

stun/

dim the light that continues through the forgotten salient the grin of it invisible nothing as before to echo of nor of to speech reclamation shat purpose & a frozen view where the dawn has frozen in the paralysis of it night cancelling all as from a view of which it is null/

silent abort…

(…ideation skinning the blackened meat from liquid bones to touch where to shadowing is the nullity of the light that pierces scald of the abortive a shit-streaked sky of vacuum breathless closure of fist unravelling to reveal the dismembered corpsal of a child where to utter merely of the dead till breathe of confetti drag hilt what sheen sickness in the lapse of grip of the sweat of the brow nothing of to claim in the reek night absence of the forgotten eye alone of wishbone trilogy as nectar to fall from the cruciform trees breakage nothingness scattering its seeds to the dead airs of memory dissolved in future tense of cold weight absolve till amber closure dragging out the tines from the skin of absenteeism nothing of the scald the dissolve of silent…)

...of the vocal echoing out where deathed tomorrows colourless & abounding throughout where the close of wound is the stench of shit detritus waste collision nocturne given to breakage a glint in vicious air as adrift in a vertigo of blindness echoing veranda of silenced of the become nothing of the will to follow onwardly where to stasis is to parallax ice in the veins of nectar lights that seek to penetrate till savour wind a landscape a nothing a breath it cannot whereof as if to say that echo-echo blind is to turn the other cheek a slap to the face a nullity of excursion severance to taste in some psychosial depth of trace what of till embers to surmount beneath the sky's chambers as shudder of throughout skinned lest of longing harvest of no end where to what sung a razor entity a silhouette upon the horizon as bloodily the partaken of the silence of breakage of skeletal dense hollow close till non-reflect in the it what seen as drag of carcass tears split the skin the absent traipse through nothing ever in a sick sunk spun/ as if to...

===================================

*(...of the blood/ of the ache of it/ of the outreaching
fingers blossoming into obsidian flowers...)*

...lightless pageantry of exigency turning in the sarcophagus night where to endless is to exit braille of the sky allwhile to dust turning in the corridors the weighted meat/

severed of the attrition silence till close of wound of terse of bloodless polka despair rent soil of a broken column a wired jaw fixed for approximation where to skin is to broken of the bodily vacant a taste of spent tears/

of the tears that flow inwardly to extinguish the candle of else dense as frozen light nothing from the which in a corrosive of speechless dead but once it murmurs spread-eagled upon the surface of some desert of bones till all but shadow of the nectar breath the absenteeism of rat's pulse a closed fist a nothingness...

as drag of toothen climate to strip the room in which it found as having taken from step -cannot- outwardly unto ever to recede... cylindrical in breathless waste of excise where of the blood floweth the knock the rapture of lights caress of some floorboards rotting away as of carcass where nothing else for the matter of which ever of the once before it/

a child's toys burning in a hearth of spent syringes of clotted blood of razor wire lack/ given taken sudden as has ever been throughout the stained glass the smear of meat…locked under by the weight of water here there once thrice twice forgotten rock paper scissors as if to say give or take an emaciation of light of cataract ever to flow…

dense as shit the reek of the delirium that speaketh of nullity & has no realm other than through the psychosial expel of nothing ever where to voiced is to bite & tear asunder through the rupture the song the adroit the semblance the simulacrum destined to undone/ as was/ so it shall/

nothing of the matter/ taken from what given in a closure of naught till darkness the gutted glut of blood & talisman the secretive the spoken of the vibrate of none where to breathe is to pageant never of the before nor else as if to cauterize what spoken of forgotten in the memory taxed by the film of the negate as throughout the misted silence the severed tongue the fingernails extracted a butcher's calm where all breathe subsides into where there was ever only of given unto absenteeism a broken lock a/ till what once/

ever of the shadowing throughout where the burnt bodies glow in ember dusts blackened by the heave of the sky's pelt reflected in the pupil of outstretch collect the…

stillness of outstretched waters collected in the night when all is absent merely of through the exigency of want where to flow is the sickness is the amphetamine salve of vibrate of tones as teeth to grind the corpse electrical illumined by…more shit than shovel…in & out of realm as is having stepped throughout switches from landscape unto cylindrical unto corridors it vibrates it no longer the knowing of through the razor's intent through the rat's colourings within the body vocal in…

as onwardly never motion of as of which a sleight of hand a breakage point a scar whereof till scarred once more the outstretched hand to touch blossoming into black dust everof till cauterize of wound never of the recall the remainder frozen as of waste shards of shrapnel sticking in the throat in an attempt to digest what cannot can only of through the night being superfluous as a shit-filled latrine a blood-stained pissoir in the abattoir of night where children beg for coinage in the lack of everything else as turning in the mire of it till seeker's claim nothing of the avaricious spitting cracked teeth into the emptiness as solarized to rupture here now & however…

solarized as if to say that to brim upon is the opiate of having discarded lights for the betterment of speechless dark the throat cut in forest of vocal emptiness burning all the while in the breach-birthed absolve where night is to endlessly in-dream of spectre collision within the recurrent roomscape given to trade with foreign in catascope reckless avalanche...

until...steps back it drag along through the words that cast bear no signs of other than...no footsteps to follow merely one singular footstep blood-stained in the centre of a snow-covered room... nothing of the dawning of... (shutter snap closed)...

taking from in onwardly till nowhereon bound for the guillotine of laughter where to circus animals carouse within an audience of cardboard cut-outs...there will be no applause...

haemorrhage of the onward step where to paralysis is the arena of night broken by foreign till expel of shadowing never of...it all falls down...twisted the limbs to balance upon a ha'penny's edge...night's reflection in the dilated pupils drifts slowly by as of silent mist...

nothing more to voice nothing of to claim nothing of till extrication stricken from the book as is said it once it said till nocturne's blood expelled through pulse bulb entity of sickness unto foreign ever of through meat dark chase a glint that refuses yet cannot some density of the rind to compare with avarice cut clear from the wound of never to dispel...

=====================================

…in silence of/ shadow bound by the never having been other than the slash-mark intent of never having been or otherwise/ tidal as blood stone cold as the reflect of rat as the pupils glaze over given to stitch the skin of it where in darkness the malign is a clarity of null a speech driven from out of step once thrice having taken/ colours to collide in the stricken wasteage of bones of flesh of meat & the reek of the ever never having as skinned till purpose shredded by sudden as if to shrift in the poverty of else where to blind-sighted is to have ever uttered/ point upon point the tidal of which cancelled out where the wound closeth & the walls melt away in the intoxication of nights long held to eclipse/ as acidic to gathered the obsidian petals of the redeem to scatter unto where bloodless the oceanic is the depth of haste of silhouettes of sharded lights/ in mimicry of the damned it stretches out as of limbs to be pierced by to be foreign as to be frozen blank waste of the occluded semblance of manifest/ shudder cold snap an echo of it in retrocede nothing of in the tension between one singular death & then another as taken from from the commence scuttle of blind of the eye's mercury cataract viewed from a distance where the mimicry expands to a singular point on a horizon of rot & nothing more/ as if it/ till warped wind in a catacomb of nocturne breath as of in blackened throughout as if to reclaim it never once a cast shadow a silent tongue torn out/ till dream once more of the cancerous the meat's abattoir opulence

where to be is to have erased till drag it cannot be erased the rat of feel where sickness of is all/ of the coffin heart spat out into a clear cold distance perhaps shit spat at the sky of depth non-ask questioning naught of it what spell of collideoscope a bitter rapturite where to dim what once forgotten as specious to depth throughout in the absence of climate bitten down upon a scream erased in mid-flight yet terse yet still to spiral echoing out from breakage point of nothing ever/ all dead it murmurs beneath the cloaked breath the ruptured silence in a nothing of what weight till cracked shell abandoned leakage of silver smoke a severed tongue a knowing of no boundary other than/ till of in the which none of in other what of expel a trace till occluded sickness to dredge in a lobotomy of silken rust the implements of speech cast off no words for the morrow the marrow nausea of tilt throughout in a given trace spoken as was before ever of the negate the dissent of breakage rupture nothing of as was spoken of/ where to be is to disembowel the pale light of harnessed to the onslaught of expel a/ absent of till trace occluded semblance of winds to speak of what dense/ it no worship/ the eyes smeared across an endless jarring wailing in the dark a shit-stained mattress a scattering of broken glass to taste winds perhaps the blood of it the essence of that screaming as of nullity cold beseech upon one knee in a genuflect a skinned blind weight nothing of the lungs that burn no shadow of a warp of the blood taken from what speech eradicted all dredged what furnace/ as through the fleshed once carousel of ever after in the irredeem of open sores in a pit of graven entrenched in a gallows' shadowing across every sunlit of the forgotten what flesh to absolve of it/ till vomiting the scars of the depth of tread what will to obscure it having forgotten the outset of the endless night where to flesh is to haven a-dream throughout the meat of traceless abandon lights/ as sun knows no worship a slash mark of striate where bitten the bones slide from out of view as flesh surmounts in echo-chamber desire/ in tint of all of the undone what shadows to recollect as a shimmering of cloud all stricken from the book to distaste a forgotten retrospect endlessly devoured silken the cut of the blood to the membrane to the silence reclaimed what once as was as was spoken of given to the reclamation else of it in a back-step into where roomscape dissolves & absent light devours in cold weight/ frozen blue mists across an evening's hallucination/ what bones to wrench from the fleshed abandon of having no other recourse than to sleep the hours of permeate nothing of the before there nor of what matter of it the/ until/ until as what was in the beginning/ stripped until nor of the spoken for silenced of the devour till speechless where to be is of the naught the erased features of it/ the eye peeled away to reveal no surface given to dispel as through what of it in the breakage of absences cast across the scene what scene of the where to be is cum upon the heavenly gardenias of silent realms/ night is very.../ nothing of the outstretched skin through the coffin realm of rat eye will stretch the taut of blood throughout where sickness of to dredge/ laceration bedamned as paring away the smeared teeth of the sky is to be without origin merely only of/ as culled the animals called ashore unto/ in a wreckage of the outspoken silenced/ flesh upon flesh/ in the shit-reek of night endless butchered as of till of nothing ever of...

(...spillage of crimson light obsidian entity as closed what wound in the bereft of...closure tongue to trace of the expel nothing of till given/ what will what of cold dice cast in a winter alleyway far from the living far from the dead/ breakage of spent bones underfoot/ a grit of teeth of silenteeism/ it what once/ nothing of the matter it handmedown solace breakage of devour it/ skinned of the once that was ruptured in a pit of bound bones of attrition anguish/ it all come down to end as was from the commence of never/ ashen promise/ nothing ever as before...)

===================================

…eye see eye/ it is said/ broken valves of teeth stricken by the momentary trace of non-percept/ black vault of the shutter it down upon breaking from nothing ever into nothing once was hilt of reckless abandon extricated flow of listless blood throughout the exposed veins of/ given as of/ not a trace of sky/ burnt black in the harlequin obscure till absenteeism sudden white shock of light to contain in the cylindrical breath of it/ as the once/ sinew closure of what speaketh now where to why is to of the absolve/ blank waste/ dim the light of the forgotten as was once forth to claim endlessly to churn of the milk teeth of some abandoned purpose/ turn out the fucking lights/ a light bulb swings as of some discarded noose in some deserted landscape from one singular gnarl of branches reaching no more for the/ a dead pelt of sickness sliding from the meat of the sun's light foreign as of/ nothing as of/ dead lock breath of insomniacal night stretching to the beyond of all that will remain unknown…

(…there or other of the spent winds carousing the etched flesh bleeding of the convulsive where to breathe is to dis-ease a stricken opulence of disrecollect…speaks as it cannot…whispering the tidal of the long forgotten that do not weep of the tears once spilled…amber light permeating throughout…dead tones… nothing of the not no longer the…as all to bleed of…an orifice in the emaciated sky…final as of which till of where children *strip the skins from the dead as if to turn where the air is electrical…colours cold dawn light…ever the light/ ever the darkened tidal of…so it was & will ever of the be that forages in the reflect of vulture's tooth where to skyline is of the abort of silenced echoes…there are yet nor will there ever be the words to acclimatize… dead tones of the retrocede…rat's piss upon a drowning flame…)*

===

…motion unto waste as the machine inverts to collide with the absent self of breath's align as colour it final stricken from the book & foreign of the taste of blood rising up through the parched throat to signify/ shadowing of it in the intent to close the door made of vapour tones an electrical storm to illuminate at will as silenced from the outset nothing of the words that do not carry merely genuflect before the nothingness/ vault snap shutter snapped down/ the warped bones sing of attendant misery where to held once uttered of was called upon forgotten ever of/ nothing to claim yet ever to expel through where fields of burnt black grasses bend in the winds as from some window a vantage point there is nothing else to of in the matter of which a semblance of dispel/ here an eye there another/ the ripped sight of it to fall writhing as upon a nullity of expire till close the wound as sleep is absent/ insomniacal density wandering from one carousel of frenzy till paranoical redempt where to be is to echo of the vibrate of ever-else no matter/ nothing escape from yet nothing to hold bound in the barbed wire of retrocede spoken as was taken from in dead tones where to rat is to withstand rolling over upon lime & shattered glass thinks nothing of the matter/ in the shit reek of promise the skulled abort suckles upon the dry bones of collapse/ fingers to trace the whispers throughout the dark what dark what light in the static absolve till terse of closure realms/ till beseech of/ no force no motion no gestural need/ as the flesh

subsides neither smeared nor butchered throughout an abattoir's murmurings through the teeth of blood lack/ staunched meat and the breakage of it given to relapse upon/ secretive that burns in the eyes of rat eye for one a traipse has not spoken through the solderded emptiness/ a broken column a frost-bitten lapse/ effortlessly cast of to taste in the regalia of tears that will not flow/ teeth the tear from the mouth of it till closure of/ endless night in the refrain a libretto a silence/ till breakage of bones nothing more to offer in the silence that scuttles through the pit of the membrane's swollen eyelids of speech a-dream/ all dead as is noted all the same/ noted the colours slide away to reveal utter dark a fist a frozen paralysis a nothing/ in the shadowing of it what wound/ ever of in the abandonment of the dead airs traceless filtering through the flesh till death it doth part/ as to where what from some psychotic aftermath/ as blackened to reveal it unto none in the what of it what come to frozen of in a slaughterhouse cheer the dis-ease of it raping the frozen orchids through which one tread/ sees then as of nothing ever of before once known a collision stripping the flesh from the echo's light as the thin circus of dispel in a fruition of amber nothingess to cauterize where to breathe is to seeker's realm of excise the weight of sudden as if to fall dragged from the kick & scream/ as one breath to champion the infinite screams through the skin of it the barren flesh of reclamation/ ever after/ breaking upon the oceanic of it where the blood lack

*it cannot/ silent all the bloody while/ vibration tones
& the sky's collapse emaciated where the voice of one
final child cries out & nothing more/ no trace redempt/
broken rusty locks a doorway forced open in the sleeping
silhouettes of the silent/ recalls the flame/ the once/ the
abort of being leaving little trace in the mockery dispel
of hyenic laughter upon/ life is very long/ sharded glass
& a cracked realm of distemper laced blood no never
as before in the dark to roundelay as once was broken
given to collapse where life is.../ as bitter the locked
jaw spills light upon till breakage of restive of unknown
paring away the deft dead tones of approximate feel/
as the noose's vague winds call ashore the silent witness
of all that could have ever been/ the lungs turned to
shit before the eyes the rotting away of it throughout
given unto slash-mark fragrances where to of what once
a kaleideoscopic of broken words fading unto the edge
of the night where to/ stun/ breakage wreckage stripping
the lack from nothing ever/ until the silence returns &
there is the shadowing of it/ seamless to touch it in the
purity of desire for the one thing other than the given
of in the/ where no willow weeps till close of ever/ a
shattered skeleton of breath throughout the rent air/
ocular roving/ in the failure of it given to expiration...*

*(...crushed bones of a silenced silhouette breaking
throughout where to be is the rat of final ever as the rot
crawls throughout the abounding parameters of nullity*

ever of till speech recollect nothing of till shale once drift
of it/ as the blood's seed scattered upon the vocal vacant
bodily of broken tones where all's to collision takeage
of the will to desist never of the other than throughout
where to be is the rat of final ever of as the night drags
its claw throughout to pare away its dying...)

===

(…a final scene of breakage harvest of the shrapnel tears the barbed wire tumbleweed that caresses the blood-specked sands/ jackal gathering shimmering in the dry heat/ plume of smoke arises lacking any origin/ there is nothing of this…)

...shall eye says it again as if to having of it once was where to absolve is to titanium streaks across a slashed canvas of intent...from the whittled bones to wash away the drought...it wishes for no longer...smears the gait of it with silhouettes...

...in damage seasons taken through the void's reduct where to blossom is to fallen haven of till slaughter of the night gouges out the be-ing of where to none transfixed through the socket's vacancy...

...as if to say if ever what were boring holes in the soil
of amber sentient nothing of the matter null...time
passes it is said...the tension between one singular act
& another is the desire for ever other than as the body
burns blackened light...

...dead tones mark the escape of breathe unto where to film of ice coat the broken body vocalized...not a chance...colours expire...light dies down...ever if as of what cannot be if merely to collect the scrags of foreign...

…indifference beneath the sun of it collapsed into thine vapour trails whereof unto…exigency of the expelled purpose…ever the naught taken from what distance spilling forth as division trace…

...*cylindrical as if to view the silent earth its gilded colours long forgotten...not a trace of...tearing screams from absenteeism to collect...a wishbone trilogy of nothing ever...lest it be in the knowledge of having never...*

...*striate of intent where to calling one ashore the candied corpses of the lapse a nocturne's emptily unspoken tines eradicated as to lack is the unto ever until no more...the hands fall to the sides as...*

...till trace redempt some animal frenzy kicking the shit veritable the teeth caved in existence in a vice of cold colours...seeking to burn of it...nothing of...through the talus lights a shiv glints/ vibrates...

...the vocal point has abandoned the meat of all soundings to collide in a vertigo of tears of blood as in the ever of what stun till disrecollect through what once stricken from the book of it what once...

...to desist...to turn aside from...to scatter the ocular cataracts to the dogs of speech fed to the marrow by it through the lock-jaw haven without end the strip & bleed of it given to expire where on is no nothing no not ever of...

(...distance to trace from the eye's focal point of un-speak as the length of it is to be discarded winds that grip the shards to draw blood...glass shatters a sneer in the half-light a search-light the blood smeared upon the walls in a vacant room far from the living far from the dead...all once was...& the turning of the screw in the skull's pageant...nothing of the ever of it as nothing of of the to & fro...awakens covered in bile of the pill-sick ideation clemency...all charred & still yet ablaze... nowhereon...nowhere ever...extraction taken from the silencing of it...entity of sickly light burning of the... nothing to having taken from where to have known is only where nothing of the utterance spreading its wings ablaze in the night allwhile burning unto to be gone... knuckles cracked...the silence will ever know & yet will show no cards...an inhalation of razor blades where to night is to drenched in amber sweat having of the rejected solace/ final as...)

===

echo tone
of burn-white ivory skin(ned)
deft shadow of
redeem in
harvest ever of the null
cold dice traces

the skyline's blood of absence
nothing of
in the break-neck
wind of
till turn what ashen
nothing ever of

ice what once
the pulse a-dream
solace nothing amber of collect
the bones of lapse rooted
rotting teeth
of once

sung aloft from dread departed
the blood of
mercury abandon &
the skull-lit
eyeline
froze weight as

fingers to trace(less)
of the null to bear lightless
the sickness of to extend
return to blood
to premise
from where all fallen

all what spoken
turned from in the glint of
in the turn of
weightless
burning ever of in
blackened tidal night

secretion ash of known
of the fallen to
the breathe of absence at the edge of
where nothing
scarlet the extraction
blood to caress

all locked the dark beneath
echo echo no
there what matter if
final edge
the burnt history rising in
the throat parched

blind fist
& the meat the
solace arbitrary silence
skinning the teeth of
nullified
collect of bone dust weight

night what lapse abort
footsteps erased
nothing of the trace
sunk weight in
distance burning recollect nothing
blank space echo

turn of blood relapse it
collect of shard
cold light
& the coil of nowhere having
not once in black veranda
vault

hands dead fallen to the edge of
blood to stone to nullify
asked of through the
grit of nothing
frozen waters flow
disgust rip

lightless pageant
lapsed in meat
traces once echo of the
uttered collect
the shadows the upturned
eye's reflect

fallen no
at pitch-white edge extend
where barbarous is
& the teeth of sting rip
shred of pulse
to the furtive dogs

long foreign rising up to slaughter
the breath
of ever having forgotten
the weight of taste
the tongue that
severed

bile blood knot at the edge
of spoken recoil
unspoken of
in the wreckage of shadowing
lock till turn
burned black

nothing of it as was once
turning to the breakage point
of amber
shit for sustenance
the turning of through the
depths of exile

black light of the abort
turn what asked of
shadows flitting the walls of ever
turn what close
breakage hollow terse
reduced to

syringe dust & the cold lock
till turn of weighted beast pregnant
with slaughter
of the tremor fingers the elected
to never
once known never

long tidal to collect the ashen
silenced by drought
a murder of vulture's teeth
extension of black meat
rank solace of the
all what having

PUBLISHED BY ERRATUM REPRINTS

The Scourge of Villanie
John Marston

Civilisation Its Cause and Cure
Edward Carpenter

www.ingramcontent.com/pod-product-compliance
Lightning Source LLC
Chambersburg PA
CBHW061458210726
48287CB00007B/2566